THE SAILOR
WHO CAPTURED
THE SEA

ALSO BY
DEBORAH NOURSE LATTIMORE

ARABIAN NIGHTS
Three Tales

THE SAILOR WHO CAPTURED THE SEA

And Other Celtic Tales

WRITTEN AND ILLUSTRATED BY

DEBORAH NOURSE LATTIMORE

🏛 HARPERTROPHY®

AN IMPRINT OF HARPERCOLLINSPUBLISHERS

The Sailor Who Captured the Sea
And Other Celtic Tales
Copyright © 2002 by Deborah Nourse Lattimore
Text for "The Sailor Who Captured the Sea"
was first published in 1991.

Library of Congress Cataloging-in-Publication Data
Lattimore, Deborah Nourse.
The sailor who captured the sea and other Celtic tales / written
and illustrated by Deborah Nourse Lattimore. — 1st Harper
Trophy ed.
p.   cm.
Contents: Sailor who captured the sea — Why the faery folk
cannot rule Scotland — Black knight of Tintagel.
Summary: Brings together a tale of the Irish Book of Kells
which, when copied, will bring lasting peace to the land;
a Scottish tale of a battle between a mortal king and the fairy
queen; and a tale from Cornwall of a knight, his lady,
and a terrible beast.
ISBN 0-06-442153-8 (pbk.)
1. Tales—Great Britain. 2. Tales—Ireland. [1. Folklore—Great
Britain. 2. Folklore—Ireland.] I. Title: Sailor who captured the
sea. II. Title: Why the faery folk cannot rule Scotland. III. Title:
Black knight of Tintagel. IV. Title.
PZ8.1+   2001024678
398.2'0941—dc21   CIP
                                                                 AC

Typography by Andrea Simkowski
❖
First Harper Trophy edition, 2002
Visit us on the World Wide Web!
www.harperchildrens.com

To my husband, Steve,
and our children, Nicholas, Isabel, and Judith,
and to all my creative friends, who persevere

CONTENTS

Author's Note

When I was young, my grandmother and I lay on a four-poster bed, on a satiny, eiderdown quilt, and there, propped up by freshly fluffed pillows, we journeyed through fairy tales from around the world. Long after my grandmother had stopped reading, I remained lost in the stories and the otherworldly illustrations. So I became familiar with castles, fairies, dragons, knights in armor, spirited damsels, and adventures that I could join anytime I picked up a book.

Now, years later, I find myself writing stories that conjure up those dreamy nights filled with enchanted places and folk. In this collection of three stories, I traveled to Ireland, Scotland, and the haunted shores of Cornwall. These places remain vivid in my memory as if I'd lived there among these people, and in turn, I have found myself transported and transformed: I have become an Irish artist escaping a Viking raid, or a fairy who wants to be a queen of Scotland, or—and this one really excites me—a ghost in full armor awaiting a terrible beast inside an ancient castle.

When I first started reading folk tales

from Ireland, I found none that spent any time at all talking about the early artists who created some of the most breathtaking art in the world. I studied how the repeated patterns and symbols wove themselves around each other. Because color, line, and patterns all tied together drive me crazy and make me want to paint and draw, I looked up more and more books in the library. Soon I was surrounded by all sorts of Irish art, and it was wonderful! Could I possibly draw anything that looked like that? And, after reading all those Irish folk and fairy tales, if I could approach this work like a novice artist (which I was when it came to drawing like this), I could make mistakes, improve, and maybe even design a book of my own that honored Irish artists. I think I did it! You might want to try some of these patterns for yourself, drawing designs around the letters of your name. That's what I did and I still do it for fun.

And when I was in the library, lost in those incredible books on Ireland, I bumped into the realm of the early Scottish kings. I didn't know very much at all about the earliest rulers. I knew names such as Bonny Prince Charlie, Robert the Bruce, and Mary, Queen of Scots. So, I began to dig into the archaeology of the Highlands. The earliest buildings were earthen mounds with moats and some had small towers for defense. I found stone circles and rows, similar to Stonehenge. I found haunted woods and mysterious pools and hollows. And then I found a rock with a single, sunken footprint in it. Immediately, I thought of King Arthur and the sword he and he alone could pull from a stone. After reading about the Scottish rock, I discovered that only true Scottish kings could put their foot into this indented spot. I'd never heard anything about it before. Now you can read my own story about it. The King and his grandsons were real people; whether or not the fairies were real is entirely up to you.

When I was on vacation in Cornwall, a local man told me about the ghosts that haunted the Western shores in Cornwall, Devon, Wales, and Ireland. As I heard one story after another, the skin along my neck shot through with chills. He took me to all the places where ghosts had been seen since the times of King Arthur and King Mark. Battling knights fill the legends of places like Slaughter Bridge, presumably the place where King Arthur was mortally wounded, or Camelford, which once claimed to be one of the king's castles, possibly Camelot itself. When a local guide's storytelling was coupled with the traveling I did in these areas, I began to imagine I saw shadowy figures dressed in armor or medieval gowns, and heard the clatter of warhorses, the clanging of invisible swords in deadly combat, and the chanting voices of long-silenced monks. It is one thing to read about these places; it is another to visit them, when you can begin to sense the presence of life gone by. There are so many adventures and episodes about the lives of the knights of the Round Table and so many more about Arthur himself, not to mention the earliest of the Cornish kings, that I needed mentally to swim in the myths, absorb their incredible varieties, and then let them spill out into the last of these three stories. I hope you go there, too. It doesn't matter if you travel by foot, plane, or book, because once you've heard just one tale, you'll thirst for more, and your dreams will take you there whenever you want to go. Never have I seen more, read more, or heard more wild and wonderful tales than in Cornwall, especially ghost stories. I believe if you look for the stories you long for, they'll come to you. Perhaps they'll even visit you at night, when you are safe in bed. I hope they do. Whether your travels take you to Ireland, Scotland, Wales, Cornwall, or Devon, may those forces of your own imagination guide you! And good reading!

THE SAILOR
WHO CAPTURED
THE SEA

In the year of the Lord 804, near the Port of Dubh-linn, there lived three brothers. Fursa, the oldest, was a strong-armed boy with a generous nature who, when he grew up, became a stonecutter. Niall, the middle brother, was a serious, quiet lad who grew up to be a metalsmith. Broghan, the youngest, went from one thing to another until he became, at last, a sailor and was happy.

One day news came that Viking ships had attacked several northern ports of Ireland. Many people fled inland to the town of Kells and the monastery of St. Columba. Fursa and Niall gathered up their few belongings.

"We are going to the monastery," said Fursa. "Come with us."

"That is fine for you and Niall," replied Broghan. "But I cannot leave the sea."

Broghan bade them farewell. But as the months passed, fewer captains braved the sea for fear of attacks by Viking ships. Broghan found less and less work. He missed his brothers. At last, he, too, set out for Kells.

After three days' walking Broghan reached the watchtower of the great monastery. Fursa himself met Broghan with an embrace and led him to the scriptorium, where holy books were copied. There Niall greeted Broghan warmly.

"We gave up our trades," Fursa explained, "and worked hard to become artists. Finishing the Great Book of Gospels is our most important task."

"According to an ancient law," he went on, "once the Book is completed, no one, not an Irish king nor a Viking lord, can attack us again."

Broghan looked at the pages spread across the tables.

"The abbot, our Master Scribe, drew these," said Fursa, pointing. "He was a farmer before he came to St. Columba. Niall and I hope one day to draw our own master pages."

"I wish I could draw such wonders," Broghan said softly.

"Here," replied Fursa. "Take up my pen."

"No," said Broghan. "I am no artist. But I will work in the fields until there is work for a sailor again."

So it was that Broghan joined his brothers at the monastery. He worked in the fields and in the vineyards and did all the things asked of him.

Soon the old abbot wished to return to his homeland on the island of Iona. Broghan took him by oxcart to the coast and helped him board his ship.

"How I love the feel of a boat!" Broghan thought, breathing the salt air. He picked up a small conch shell, held it to his ear, and listened to its ocean murmur. And though the breeze tugged at his sleeves, Broghan slowly turned back toward Kells, the shell nestled in his cloak.

With the abbot now gone, Fursa became the Master Scribe.

"Come, Broghan," said Fursa. "It is time you practiced with your pen. We must finish the Book of Gospels quickly and will need everyone's help."

"I am a sailor, not a scribe," Broghan said, shaking his head.

"Help us," said Niall. "You will find, as did I, that your hand grows surer with practice."

But try as he might, Broghan could not draw as well as his brothers. One day he slipped away and walked toward the sea. In the lowland mists he listened vainly for the calls of seabirds and imagined the sea brimming with ships. "Soon I'll be on a ship again, where I belong," Broghan said to himself, and he held the conch shell to his ear.

The next day word came that the old abbot had died in his sleep on Iona. Fursa put down his pen, took up his chisel, and carved a stone cross in the abbot's memory. Weeks later, when it was completed, the monks raised it on its foundation. Suddenly a shout came from the watchtower. The king of Tara appeared at the gate.

"War is expensive," he told the monks. "My men need gold for their purses and meat to fill their stomachs." He motioned to his soldiers, who rushed to the fields to herd the cattle.

"Wait!" said Fursa. "The animals you may take. But whatever treasure we have belongs to God and this monastery."

Then the king spied the great stone cross.

"Let the man who carved this cross come to my castle to be my stonecutter. In exchange I will allow your monastery to stand."

Fursa knew that many other monasteries had been burned to the ground by invading kings. He embraced his brothers and left.

"We must finish the Great Book quickly," said Niall, "before the king of Armagh comes to Kells, as he surely will." He set himself to the task.

Broghan saw that Niall was even a better Master Scribe than Fursa. And though the drawings were different, both styles were strong and beautiful. The more Broghan tried to copy them, the more mistakes he made. Finally, one night, Broghan threw his drawings into the fire. He changed into his sailor's clothing and stormed out the monastery gate.

"What good is a sailor so far from his ship?" he said to himself angrily. "It is all well and good for my brothers to fashion pictures that look like worked stone or metal. No one can make parchment into sea."

When Broghan felt the cool sand beneath his feet, he scanned the horizon for a ship.

"A Viking boat," yelled a villager running up the shore.

Broghan saw a small, battered boat,

its mainmast cracked, pitch violently over the waves. A young boy clung to the lines. Without hesitation Broghan flung himself into the crashing surf. He swam to the boat and climbed on. He tied up the mast and guided the boat to shore.

Broghan saw that the boy was not hurt. He covered him with his cloak and built a good fire.

"This is the carving of a king's boat," thought Broghan, touching the deeply cut patterns on the prow. Then a glint of light caught his eye. There, on the floor of the boat, was a broadsword. Broghan had saved one of the enemy. He thought of his brother and the Great Book and the real danger they now faced. But this was only a boy.

"Come, lad," he said abruptly. "You've

drifted off course."

Broghan pushed the boat to the water's edge, and soon it carried its young master beyond the cresting waves.

Broghan hastened back to Kells to warn Niall and the others. But it was Brother Donnan who descended the watchtower to meet him.

"Thank God you have returned," said Brother Donnan. "The king of Armagh came, and Niall went with him to do service as his metalsmith. What shall we do?"

"You will keep a good watch for Vikings," said Broghan. "And I will try to finish the Great Book."

Broghan picked up his pen and began to draw. This time, instead of trying to draw like Fursa or Niall, he thought of the sea. Slowly and awkwardly at first, then more easily, with a thin, light line, he soon completed page after page.

Many days passed until the silence of the scriptorium was broken by the urgent calls of Brother Donnan. Ivar, king of the Norsemen, had arrived. Broghan did not stop until he heard heavy footsteps in the hall. Then he laid down his pen and faced the Viking, whose great fame seemed to fill the room. Amidst the unfinished pages lay Broghan's work, the paint still wet.

"I know this design," said King Ivar, looking closely at one page. "It is like the pattern I myself carved into the prow of my son's boat. Not long ago I thought he was lost—yet he came back to me." Ivar turned toward Broghan.

"Hold out your arms," he said.

Broghan raised his arms. King Ivar drew his sword and gently laid it across Broghan's outstretched arms.

"Even though you have not finished your Great Book, I surrender my weapon to you for saving my son. Your monastery is safe." Then the king and all his men left.

Of the three brothers from Dubh-linn, Broghan alone remained at the monastery and finished the Great Book. He had only to look at his brothers' drawings to feel their presence clearly.

And never again did he miss the sea.

Why the Faery Folk Cannot Rule Scotland

In the very early days of the Scottish realm, many fierce chieftains battled across the land to see who would be king. The strongest of these was David of Carlisle. With his son, Henry, and cousins Angus and Duncan at his side, David drew out his weighty claymore and cut a path through each and every clan. Just as victory seemed to be his, David saw fresh warriors descend from the north.

"I cannot fight all at once," he called out. "If I could stay them back long enough to finish here, we could take them."

"I'll go up, Father!" said Henry. And he waved his own men on. But no sooner did they go than a lance struck Henry down dead.

"Henry! My own dear son!" shouted David. He stood up in his saddle and raised his arm over his head. "I swear and pledge that whosoever helps me stop those villains shall share my crown!"

David and his army swung around, and in all four directions they bolted, weapons drawn, and a great skirmish ensued. Then, out of the trees, a silent, solitary figure appeared and pointed a long, thin finger toward the northern hills.

Suddenly a bright, white mist flooded the glen. It rose like a curtain, then an ocean, swirling and shaping itself until it took on the appearance of a woman's face, head thrown back and laughing like a fiend. Twisting and floating upward, it completely circled the foe. They ran into one another in great confusion, not knowing comrade from enemy, nor horse from man. Claymores and spears clanged and cracked until, exhausted, the enemy threw themselves down in the dirt and surrendered.

As the mists cleared, David stood on the ancient rock of Dunadd, where all true kings of Dal Riada place their foot. As his foot met the stone, it pushed down into the rock, leaving a deep, stoney impression. It was by this very footprint, prophesied in ages past, that Scotland now had its true king, brave, strong, and wise. So it was that David became king with his foot squarely set on the rock of Dunadd.

Grand celebration and merriment followed. The Great Hall nearly burst with clansmen from all parts of Scotland. Peace was made between them. For every man who had fought on that day, King David gave out lands and beasts, titles and deeds and purses of gold. His cousin Angus was now the Earl of Ross, and his cousin Duncan, the Earl of Fife.

"Now I have rewarded all, save the creeping mists! Let us drink to peace and to my two grandsons, Malcolm the Fair and William the Lion, who shall rule after me."

Cheering echoed from one end of the great hall to the other, but there was one voice that didn't cheer. Muttering and cursing came from the throat of a woman. Tall and strange, she was dressed from head to toe in purple heather from the glens, moonstones ran around her brow, and over all she wore a cloak of thistles.

"Who be ye?" said King David, his cup half raised.

"Do ye not know me then?" she answered. "It was I, Queen Maeve, who cast the spell of the fogs around your enemies. Now I want my reward. You swore it on your crown!"

King David leapt to his feet. Only a sorcerer or a witch could conjure up a mist to confound a battling foe. He stared

hard at Queen Maeve and as his eyes tilted low, he saw that her feet were not on the ground. She was hovering in the air!

"If you are a Queen, where is your realm?" asked King David.

"I am Queen of the Faery Folk. Is it not true that with my help in battle, you won your crown? And did you not swear that whoever came to your aid would share that crown?"

"Here!" shouted King David. "What you say looks to be true. But you cannot be my Queen for I am already wed. Ask for some other reward. As for ruling Scotland, only human beings, not faery folk, will ever do that!"

Queen Maeve cast her dark glaring eyes upon the King, then his Queen, and then, with a small, deceptive smile, she looked at Malcolm and William, King David's grandsons.

"Those be fine laddies," said Queen Maeve. "And even though they are young, time is nothing to me. I can wait for one to be my husband. So, I'll take two rewards, one lad for the battle, the other one for the insult you did me!" With a wave of her hand, Queen Maeve swept the boys to her side and flew straight out of the great hall amid a haze of purple faery dust, leaving the broad doors banging with an ear-deafening thunder.

In an instant King David and his men rushed to arms. The bridge dropped and a brilliant army on horseback raced toward the faery glen. In minutes they found themselves in the center of a grove of oak trees that were all twisted and entwined like the tower keep of a castle. King David sat holding his horse's reigns tightly in his left hand, and brandished his claymore in his right.

"Come, Queen Maeve. Do battle with a man, not his wee laddies!"

Queen Maeve's wicked laughter resounded through the trunks and boughs to the very ends of the leaves, and the dusty faery winds followed the sound, whipping and whirling, until the horses shuddered, reared up, and cast off the warriors. King David alone sat firmly on his mount.

"Is that the best you can do, then? Scare horses?" shouted King David.

"I can do much more!" Queen Maeve

shouted back through the leaves.

"Yes, and you do it from the stealth of enchantment. My men and I, our arms and horses, are in plain view. But you, you are afraid to show your own face!"

"I fear nothing!" said Queen Maeve, and she emerged from the trees, her faery army behind her. As they were faery folk, they stood as small as children beside their Queen and even though they numbered greatly, King David thought he saw his grandsons, Malcolm and William, in the crowd, held far apart from the others.

"Queen Maeve, this fight is between you and me. Not children!"

"Be not mistaken about my army," replied Queen Maeve. "Small though they seem, they are full-grown. Let us do battle and the winner shall rule Scotland!"

With a forward thrust of his sword, King David signaled his men. A shower of spears whistled through the air, aimed at the front of the faery guard. But before they could reach the Queen's men, Maeve and her faery folk took heather from their sleeves and scattered it around. As the spears and heather met, they all turned into purple garlands and felt softly to the earth.

King David next called his archers and they, like the lancers before them, took up their weapons. They arched their bows, and a multitude of arrows left the cords. Quickly Queen Maeve took the moonstones from around her brow, and there were hundreds. She and her faery folk let them fall and rise in the air like a light rain, dropping and yet again coming. And all the while they whispered a faery spell. So wondrously did the moonstones sparkle that they dazzled the eyes of the King's men. The arrows themselves stopped in midair followed by a terrible silence. The King turned in his saddle and saw that all his men, each and every one of them, was stuck in place, eyes wide open, enchanted by the spell of Queen Maeve's jewels.

"Ay! You are powerful indeed!" said King David. "Trickery and spells are your weapons. But it will take more than heather and moonstones to rule this land. Truth, wit, and bravery be mine."

"What does that matter?" laughed Queen Maeve. "We've got you and we've got your wee laddies, too. Can you now deny that I am the more powerful and by rights should rule this land?"

King David looked at all the faery folk gathered around Queen Maeve. Something caught his eye. It was Malcolm and William, pinned back amidst the others, and very nearly impossible to see, save the fact that they had their feet on the ground and none other did, neither the faeries nor their Queen. The two boys motioned with their eyes to look down. King David saw that every delicate, slippered, faery toe hovered just above the ground but did not touch it. Then he remembered the moment he first saw Queen Maeve in the Great Hall, and how she, too, didn't touch the ground.

"I speak only the truth," replied King

David. "I should think that you, a Queen of all the faery folk and their lands, would be proud to rule such a huge kingdom. But, still, if it's Scotland you want, then hear me: let us all go to Argyll. Whosoever puts their foot firmly into the sunken mark on the rock of Dunadd, let that person wear the crown."

"Done!" said Queen Maeve.

King David felt himself lifted from his horse by the host of faery folks. They flew, wings all afluttering and humming, and along with them, not so well hidden as before, were his laddies, Malcolm and William. In no time they were all at the great rock of Dunadd.

A fight broke out among the faeries. They all pushed and shoved, each wanting a turn at the rock. But try as they might, their little feet could not touch the ground. All this time Queen Maeve laughed, throwing her head back and holding her sides. But as the last of the faeries tried and then failed to place his foot squarely upon the rock, she suddenly saw what the King was trying to do.

"This is a trick of yours!" she shouted.

"Nay, 'tis no trick, Queen Maeve," replied King David. "'Tis but a true prophecy from the oldest of soothsayers that the true ruler of Scotland must put a foot squarely into that place."

Queen Maeve stood out from her folk. Her jeweled brow and heathered collar fluttered in the wind. She held back the edges of her thistled cloak, raised her delicate foot, and placed it over the footprint in the rock. But try as

she might, she could not touch the ground. She shrieked and muttered and whispered spells, but to no avail. She could not do it.

"Fie! Fie on you, King of nothing. Let me see you put your naked foot on this place! For if you are wearing a boot, how can I see that you are square upon it?"

With that, Queen Maeve took her thistled cloak and cast it over the rock. Thick and prickly was the rock, the earth, and the land all around. King David eyed his grandsons and, taking off his boots, walked over the thistles. Even though they were sharp and painfully cut his feet, he went straight up to the rock and squarely placed his foot on the spot and held it there for all to see.

"Fine and forever, you be the King!"

shouted Queen Maeve. "But the laddies will always be mine! They have lived with me and now are become faeries."

"Not so, Maeve!" thundered King David. "I have seen all but two of your folk try to put their feet upon the rock. If it is true that Malcolm and William have become faeries, then they shall be yours. But, if they can put their foot on this rock, then they shall come back to me and share my crown after I am gone."

Queen Maeve sprinkled crushed heather over the boys' heads, dropped a moonstone into each's pocket, and parted a path in the thistles, not wanting to hurt such tender toes.

Malcolm and William went to the rock, and even though Maeve had done her oldest and strongest spells on them to make them faery folk, still they stood firmly upon the rock and took turns putting their feet into the King's mark.

"Faery folk indeed!" bellowed King David. "My laddies have come back to me, as all good Scottish sons should. As your King, I bid you adieu, Queen Maeve! As your reward for helping me in battle, you may keep your crown, your heather, moonstones, and thistles. And in your honor, whenever one of my men achieves a great place in my court, a cape of thistles shall he wear!"

Screeching and cursing, Queen Maeve and all her retinue flew away, deep into the glens, forests, up crags, and down headlands, across all Scotland. And as time wore on, as sure it must, and old King David left this earth, his grandsons,

Malcolm and William, in turn, ruled the land. And from that day to this, even though Queen Maeve is still the Faery Queen and hard to see, every time the heather blooms, a moonstone sparkles, or a thistle blows in the tall grasses, they say one of the faery folk is passing by.

THE
BLACK KNIGHT
OF TINTAGEL

O nce, across the wild westlands, over the broad reaches of moor and crag, there rode upon a great charger a knight. From head to toe, he wore a suit of black armor, deeper in color than the midnight sky with the glint and shine of the stars above his head.

Slowly he rode his horse, up and up a winding, rocky path, to the Cornish coast

and a ruined castle made magic by the play of fog and mist among its tattered walls. When he had found the darkest, most hidden place, he dismounted and lay himself down to rest.

Now, this knight did not know that a pair of deep and sparkling black eyes watched him in wonder. They belonged to Morgenna, the ebony-haired daughter of one Richard, the duke of Cornwall. She, too, had been out upon the moors, and when she saw this knight, she followed him from a safe distance.

Up the rough road Morgenna climbed until she crossed under the arch of the ruins. But when she at last arrived at the cliff, neither knight nor horse could be seen. So she sat down in the damp grass and lit a furze fire.

"Imagine, to have seen such a figure as a knight all in black! What a fancy has visited my eyes!" said Morgenna. "Still, perhaps a bit of smoke will conjure up his image again!" She laughed as the little crackling flames sparked up in short spurts, flecks of fire against the starry night sky.

Without any warning, a wild howling scream shattered the stillness, as if the moor itself were baying. Morgenna froze in her place and shut her eyes tight.

"Preserve me! Keep me safe from such animals as these might be!" she whispered without moving from her place.

"I shall keep thee safe," came a voice.

When Morgenna opened her eyes, there stood the black knight, rising up in front of her, as real as the rock itself.

For moments, Morgenna and the knight stared at each other while the baying faded into the dark.

"Who are you and where are you from?" asked Morgenna.

"I am from England," he replied. "I was one of three knights sent to kill the Questing Beast. The other two, the Red and the Green, are dead, killed by this beast. I alone escaped, mortally wounded. I knew from an ancient sorcerer that if I could find this place, I would come back to health. This is what has saved me."

The knight held out the scabbard of a sword. Its golden patterns were interlaced with jewels that glittered in his hands as if burning from a fire within.

"This scabbard once held Caliburn,

the sword of the great king. It can heal any wound it is laid upon, even that unto death. The beast knows I have it and he will try to find me."

"What does this beast look like?" asked Morgenna, shivering.

"He is a shape-shifter," said the knight. "He can change from the likeness of a man to the likeness of a bird or any other living thing he chooses. But when he is enraged, his true shape is thus formed: His head is a serpent, his body a leopard, he has a lion's hind flanks and a hart's feet. From his mouth comes the sound of forty baying hounds, and a breath as foul as a stagnant marshpit."

"If he can change his shape as you say he can, how could you know him when you see him?" Morgenna asked.

"When his piercing black eyes behold mine own, I shall know him," replied the knight. Then he frowned at Morgenna and sighed.

"What is the matter?" she asked.

"You are gifted with deep, black eyes, and for a moment, they reminded me of something," he said. "But it is nothing. And now, before you are missed, you should go. Be careful. Trust no one. The shape-shifter may be near."

Morgenna hastened to her home and stabled her horse. Her heart was full of love for the handsome stranger. She knew she had to see him again and so she did, under stealth of night. Each time she sat and made a furze fire and each time, when the knight appeared, they pledged their love. But when Morgenna told the knight that the frightful howling had come right into her village, he told her to leave.

"Venture here no more, my love, for the Questing Beast is now very close by. Come to me only if you need the scabbard, for I have shown you and you alone where it is hidden."

Now on that night, when Morgenna slipped quietly into the hall, her father, the duke, was waiting for her.

"Where have you been, daughter?" he asked.

"Only out riding," Morgenna replied.

"What's this?" said her father, grabbing her sleeve. "The smell and smudge-burn of a furze fire from the sea cliffs! Were you with someone? Who meets you so secretly in the night?"

"There is no one," said Morgenna. "I was out alone."

"I do not believe you, girl," he said. "We shall talk of this tomorrow. Meanwhile, do not leave this house or your room, until you tell me everything."

The duke's great steps stole off and the door slammed shut, its bolt clanging tightly against the wood.

Morgenna could not sleep. When her eyes shut, she saw nothing but visions of the knight and the frightful beast in combat. She arose, still sleeping, and stood at her window, when suddenly a raven flew up, cawing and scratching the pane, its feet stained with blood. It opened its beak and spoke.

"Take me to my master, the Black Knight!"

By now it was very nearly dawn and as the nighttime melted with the first rays of light, the raven quickly turned away, howled, and swooping upward, flew away.

In the morning, the duke summoned Morgenna. There was trouble in the fields.

"Last night, someone or something attacked our sheep," he said, eyeing her. "Did you hear or see anything?"

Morgenna stared hard into her father's dark eyes.

"A huge raven came at my window, and it called out to me. It had blood on its feet!" she replied

"Posh! A nightmare visited you, nothing more! But some of our sheep were killed by a wild beast in the night and *that* is no nightmare. I think it might have been your stranger. Tell me where he is."

"I know of no stranger," replied Morgenna.

The duke sent Morgenna back to her room and locked the door. That night, as on the night before, she dreamt of terrible battles on the cliff. As before, she stood up and went to her window and opened it, still sleeping but with her eyes open, as if enchanted. This time, instead of a raven, a fox appeared, his paws stained with blood.

"Take me to my master, the Black Knight," called the fox.

Morgenna tried to shake off her sleepiness and for a few moments she thought to climb out the window. But the sun began to break on the fields, and as it did, the fox turned quickly, howled, and ran away.

In the morning the duke summoned Morgenna as before.

"And now will you tell me who this stranger is," asked the duke, "now that something has been at our chickens?"

But Morgenna could only tell of another nightmare.

"Are you not frightened by these evil forebodings?" asked her father. "Perhaps if, instead of chickens, your much-beloved horse were attacked, you would tell me."

When her father spoke these words, Morgenna was indeed frightened. But if it was the Questing Beast that lurked in the night, she knew no one but the Black Knight could stop it. If only he would come break the silence and tell her father the truth!

On the following night, more nightmares filled Morgenna's dreams. This time, she awoke and heard a terrible sound outside. She opened the window and ran to the stables. There, on the straw, lay her beloved horse, dead. Standing over it was her own father, wiping blood from his hands.

"Now will you tell me!" he shouted.

Morgenna, weeping, turned to her father and spoke.

"I cannot believe that anyone I know could do such a horrible thing!" said Morgenna. And with that she ran out into the moor. For hours she wandered, wondering if the Black Knight himself were the dreadful Questing Beast. She had to know the answer.

At nightfall, a cloaked Morgenna left

her house and took great care to see that none followed her. She kept away from the well-known paths. With fear and excitement pulsing in her veins, she plunged through briar and bramble, field and thicket, until the opening to the path up the cliffs was before her. Rushing up the rocks, she found herself breathless at the ruined arch of the old castle.

"Why have you come?" came the voice of the Black Knight. "It is not safe for you to be here."

"My horse! Someone or something killed my horse and I had to discover the truth!"

"Aye, my love! It is as I feared. The Questing Beast is nearby. And now that you have come again, the beast will find me and the truth will be shown to you in bloody combat," said the Black Knight. "Go! Go quickly, lest you fall upon his path!"

Shaking with fright, Morgenna fled the ruins. As the morning lights tipped the rooftop of her home, she fell senseless onto her bed and did not awake until the following night. Little did she know that her father had followed her during the night and was planning his revenge.

Another night descended and a cloaked figure walked to the cliffs, up the path to the old stone arch. Morgenna arose to see that her own cloak was missing. It frightened her. She did not understand why, but she knew she had to return to the Black Knight and quickly. The first minute she saw the cliff she also saw the cloaked figure speaking to the Black Knight. As she drew nearer, she saw that it was her own likeness that stood there.

"Why did you not light the furze fire?" the Black Knight said.

"Because that is not myself, for here I am!" shouted Morgenna. "The Questing Beast has taken my form!"

At that very second, the figure raised a dagger and struck the Black Knight, who yelled out in anguish and pain. But he raised his broadsword and with both hands smote the shadowy figure.

Now enraged, the Questing Beast showed its true form. Its snakelike head and features writhed and struck at the knight. Its leopard and lion body lunged and shook. And its quick feet trampled the ground until it, too, shook.

Morgenna saw that both were wounded. She ran, turned over a flagstone, and brought out the golden scabbard.

"My love, I have the scabbard!" she called out.

The Questing Beast stopped in its tracks and looked Morgenna straight in the eyes. A horrible chill ran through her. She knew those eyes!

With his broadsword right before him, the Black Knight made his move; he ran the beast through.

"Morgenna!" called the beast. "Daughter! Save me!"

"This is the shape-shifter, not your father. Your true father is on the Crusade and this beast took his place, waiting for this moment!" the Black Knight called out,

his hands holding his own dire wounds.

Morgenna stood still. She looked at the scabbard glittering in the moonlight.

"How can I know what to do? Save the one I love and betray my own father? Save my father, only to find that he is not real, and let my love die? I cannot decide!"

And before either the beast or the knight could reach for her, Morgenna ran to the cliff's edge and plunged off into the blue-black ocean below.

And that was the end of all three, the brave Black Knight, the evil Questing Beast, and the beautiful ebony-haired beauty, Morgenna. But when the full moon rises and there is a foggy mist flooding the ruined walls, ghost to ghost, they come together again: the Black

Knight to watch and guard, the Questing Beast to howl and bay. And Morgenna? When a rogue wave leaps upward, black water upon the cliff, riding the crest is Morgenna, her feet atop its foam, and in her arms is a scabbard, interlaced with gold and jewels, and whoever can grasp it from her keeping surely will live forever.